A gift for

_____

Pippin
the Christmas Pig

BY JEAN LITTLE

ILLUSTRATED BY WERNER ZIMMERMANN

SCHOLASTIC PRESS ✦ NEW YORK

LIBRARY OF CONGRESS CATALOGING-IN-PUBLICATION DATA
Little, Jean, 1932-
Pippin the Christmas pig / by Jean Little ; illustrated by Werner
Zimmermann.— 1st ed.   p. cm.
Summary: Intimidated and dejected by the other animals' stories about the important gifts brought by their ancestors to the
stable where Jesus was born, Pippin the pig performs an act of kindness and discovers the true meaning of Christmas giving.
ISBN 0-439-65062-3 (alk. paper)
[1. Pigs—Fiction. 2. Christmas—Fiction. 3. Gifts—Fiction. 4. Animals—Fiction.] I. Zimmermann, H. Werner, ill.
II. Title. PZ7.L7223 Pi 2004 [E]—dc22 2003022486

10 9 8 7 6 5 4 3 2 1   04 05 06 07 08

Printed in Singapore   46
First American edition, October 2004

The paintings for this book were created in watercolor and pencil on Arches Watercolor paper.
The text was set in JoannaMT. The display was set in P22Kane. Book design by Yvette Awad and Marijka Kostiw

THIS STORY IS FOR MAGGIE JEAN SMART,

MAY 14, 2002, A VERY SPECIAL GIRL.

—J.L.

———————————————

DEDICATED TO ISABELLA L.A. KENSINGTON,

FRIEND AND MUSE.

—W.Z.

Pippin gazed up at Noddy, the grumpy old donkey. "Noddy, you look all excited," she said.

"Of course I'm excited," said Noddy. "It's Christmas tomorrow."

"What's Christmas?" Pippin asked.

"What's Christmas?" Noddy repeated. "Don't be pig-ignorant, Pippin. Everyone knows about Christmas."

The tips of Pippin's ears went very pink.

"Surely you remember that my family gave the first gift," Noddy went on. "The baby's mother rode on a donkey all the way to Bethlehem. Christmas couldn't even begin until she got there."

The curl went out of Pippin's tail. "Nobody told me a thing about Christmas," she said.

"My mother said they were almost late because of that slowpoke donkey,"

Bess said. "My great-great-great-grandmother gave her manger for the baby's

bed. Without her, the baby would have had to sleep on the floor. The best

present was the manger."

"What baby? What manger?" Pippin begged. Nobody noticed her.

"And I still don't know what Christmas is," she said.

"The hay in that manger was full of prickles," muttered Curly. "They would have scratched the child's face. One of my family had to give the mother a lamb's fleece to cushion the rough bed. The soft wool was a welcome gift, I can tell you."

Pippin's ears were now bright pink. "But where were the *pigs*?" she

demanded in her biggest voice.

"Don't fret, Pippin," Bess said. "Christmas has nothing to do with pigs.

What present could a pig possibly give a baby anyway, especially a baby as

special as that one?"

"If there were donkeys and cows and sheep, there must have been pigs,"

Pippin stated.

Once again, nobody paid any attention to her.

"My VERY-GREAT-grandparents sang him to sleep," said Coo Roo the pigeon. "That crowd of angels and shepherds kept him awake until my family crooned a lullaby. That song was of the first importance that night."

Pippin stamped her tiny hoof. "But what did the *pigs* do?" she said. "They must have been there and done something."

"No pigs were there," the others scoffed. "The very idea! The child was a king. That holy stable was no place for pigs."

Then Bess spoke up. "Pippin, face it. What could pigs have given a holy child? Pigs have nothing worthy."

Pippin hung her head. The barn door stood open a crack. Slowly, she went toward it.

Then she pushed it farther open with her snout. She had to get away.

Once outside, she waited. They might call her back.

Nobody called. They had not even noticed her leaving.

"I'm going where pigs matter but Christmas doesn't," Pippin announced

in a shaking voice. "And I won't come back! Never, ever."

As she set out, a gust of wind struck her full in the face. Snowflakes

stung her eyes and frosted the tips of her ears. She almost fled right

back inside, but she forced herself to go forward.

The cold was bitter. Soon Pippin could no longer see the barn through

the whirling snow. She passed a tattered scarecrow who stared and waved

one ragged arm at her.

Farther on, she saw a blue jay with its feathers all blown backward. The

hunched bird was too miserable to warn the world of the little pig's passing.

Pippin's feet hurt and her tail stiffened into a curly icicle.

"I will freeze out here," she whimpered, stumbling on. "If I don't turn back,

I will perish."

But she had sworn never to go back. They didn't want her. They had said

pigs were good for nothing.

At long last, Pippin reached the main road. She peered up at the mailbox

and wished she could climb inside. But she passed it and kept going.

Down the road, she stopped to catch her breath. Through the snow she

glimpsed a woman coming toward her, carrying a baby in her arms.

Pippin moved closer for a better look. The woman staggered. She wore no

gloves or hat, and her jacket was thin. And the little child, so sound asleep

that her head nid-nodded on her mother's shoulder, looked too heavy for her

to carry much farther.

"Poor things," Pippin murmured, forgetting her own troubles for a moment.

"Shhh," the woman crooned to her baby. "We have so far to go. But maybe we can find a nice warm barn to rest in." She shivered.

Pippin knew where to find a warm barn. She had sworn never to return there, but this was an emergency. "Follow me," she grunted, and she nudged the woman along the road until they came to the long farm lane.

Maybe the wind had dropped, for Pippin felt a little warmer. Even the scarecrow's smile looked friendlier.

At the barn door, the little pig pushed ahead. "Listen to me," she called

to the animals.

"Don't interrupt, Pippin," said Noddy. "We're making Christmas plans."

"I don't care," Pippin yelled. "Whatever Christmas was, it was long ago.

I have a baby here who needs a place to sleep *right now*."

Bess's jaw dropped when she saw the woman clutching her child.

"It's Christmas all over again," the woman whispered as she entered

the barn. Gently she laid her baby girl down in the manger's sweet hay.

The baby curled up and started sucking her thumb.

"Bless you, little pig. It is warm here," the woman murmured, settling

onto a nearby heap of hay. "Warm and safe."

"My word," Coo Roo whispered a moment later, "they're both asleep

already."

Then all the animals turned to Pippin.

"Who is this woman?" snapped Curly.

"Pippin, we can't take in some homeless nobody," Noddy added.

"My very-great —" Bess began.

"We'll need milk," said Pippin. "We'll need some warm, soft wool.

We'll need your old blanket, Noddy. We'll need lots of lullabies. Your VERY-GREAT-

grandparents aren't here. You must help this baby yourselves."

"But that's not a special baby," Noddy protested.

"Of course she is," said Pippin. "All babies are special."

Noddy gazed into the small sleeping face.

"You are right," he said. "I'd forgotten."

When the farmer and his wife came out to feed their animals, they saw the young woman, covered with Noddy's old blanket, asleep in the hay. Then they caught sight of the baby girl lying in the manger.

"It's Christmas," the man said softly. "Right here in our barn. It's a miracle."

"Hush," his wife whispered. "Let them sleep. We'll keep watch and see if they need our help later on."

When the couple left, Pippin looked around and saw what they had seen: Noddy's warm blanket, Curly's soft wool, Bess's manger and milk.

Pippin's tail drooped. "You were right," she said. "None of these gifts is from me. Pigs really do not have anything to give. Thank you all for being so kind to them."

The other animals looked down at the little piglet.

"Oh, Pippin, don't you see?" Bess said softly. "You gave us our very own Christmas. You gave us a chance to give *ourselves* instead of boasting about our grandparents. That was the best gift of all."

"It took a runty pig," laughed Noddy, "to teach us what Christmas is."